The Ugly Duckling

Louis Weber, C.E.O.
Publications International, Ltd.
7373 North Cicero Avenue
Lincolnwood, Illinois 60646

Permission is never granted for commercial purposes.

Manufactured in the U.S.A.

8 7 6 5 4 3 2 1

ISBN 1-56173-912-X

Cover illustration by Sam Thiewes

Book illustrations by Susan Spellman

Story adapted by Jane Jerrard

HTS BOOKS
AN IMPRINT OF FOREST HOUSE™
School & Library Edition

Once there was a little farm, with a pond full of geese and ducks.

On a fine morning in May, a duck sitting on her nest full of eggs felt something start to move underneath her . . . *crack, crack, crack.*

"Peep, peep!" Her eggs were beginning to hatch. She was very glad, for it seemed as though she had been sitting on the nest for a long, long time.

One by one, her ducklings broke through their eggshells, and each was fluffier and softer than the one before. Finally, the last egg started to crack open. It was a very big egg, and the duckling that came out was large and clumsy and a dirty gray color. He did not look like the other ducklings at all!

The mother duck thought, "How big and ugly this duckling is!" But she loved him just the same. And when she led her babies to the pond, the ugly duckling swam just as well as the rest, so she didn't worry about him any longer.

The next day, the duck took her babies to the farmyard for the first time. The proud mother duck lined her ducklings up in a neat row—with the ugly duckling at the very end—and told them to quack properly and bow their heads to everyone they met.

When the duck family entered the farmyard where the plump chickens, ducks, and geese were gathered, the other ducks were quite rude.

"Look at that ugly little fellow! He's not one of us!" said one snowy white duck. And a mean old goose even reached out and bit the ugly duckling on the neck.

"Leave him alone!" cried the mother duck. But the other birds continued to tease the poor duckling. Soon, even his own little brothers and sisters were calling him "ugly duckling," and they wouldn't play with him.

As the days passed, the duckling grew bigger and uglier. The teasing and bullying got worse and worse. Finally, he decided to run away. The duckling wandered through overgrown fields, often frightening the little birds who lived there.

"They think I'm ugly, too," he sighed.

On he went, until he came to a swamp where wild geese lived. Since he was too tired to go any farther, he stayed there for the night. The wild geese found him in the morning.

"What kind of bird are you?" they asked. But before he could answer, some men came with their dogs and frightened the geese away. The poor ugly duckling hid in the grasses, for he was too frightened to leave.

As soon as he was sure the dogs were gone, the lonely little duckling set off again, looking for somewhere to live. At last, he came to a crooked little hut, where an old woman lived with her cat and her prized hen. She took the duckling in, hoping he would grow fat so she could sell him at market.

But the cat and the hen thought themselves wonderful creatures and were very rude to the duckling. Besides, he was a wild bird, and although the hut was warm and dry, he longed to be out on the water, diving down among the weeds.

So one fall day, the duckling decided to run away and find a lake.

nd find one he did. He was happier on the lake, though the wild ducks there never spoke to him. They thought he was too ugly to bother with.

One day at sunset, a flock of beautiful birds flew overhead. Their feathers were so white they glowed, and their necks were long and graceful. The sight of them made the ugly duckling cry, though he did not know why.

Soon afterward, the wild ducks flew off. They knew that winter was coming. The duckling stayed in the lake as it got colder and colder. It grew so cold one night that the duckling awoke to find his feet frozen in a sheet of ice!

Luckily, a farmer found the duckling held fast there and broke the ice to free him. The kind farmer took the duckling home, thinking the odd bird would make a fine pet for his children.

But when the farmer set the duckling down in his kitchen, the noisy children frightened the bird, and the duckling flew right into a pail of milk and spilled it. From there, he ran across a plate of butter and knocked over a bowl of flour. What a mess he made!

The farmer's wife chased the duckling right out the kitchen door.

The frightened duckling did not run very far, for it was dark and cold outside. He knew the icy pond was not a safe place to spend the winter, so he found a hiding place behind the empty barnyard and made a nest for himself.

The ugly duckling spent the whole winter there, trying to keep warm. He came out only to search for food. It was the longest, loneliest winter he could imagine.

Spring came at last! The ugly duckling stretched his neck and tried to fly. How strong his wings were! How easily he landed on his little lake!

*J*ust as the ugly duckling was enjoying his first swim of the spring, three snowy swans appeared from the grasses along the shore. The duckling felt the same strange excitement he had felt when he had first seen them flying overhead.

He wanted to be near them so much that, even though he was sure they would treat him cruelly, he swam toward them. As he drew near, he bowed his head, ready for the name-calling and biting he had learned to expect from other birds.

But when he lowered his head, what do you think he saw? A fourth swan, the most beautiful of all, was looking back at him from the water. It was his own reflection!

You see, over that long winter, the ugly duckling had grown up. He was not a duckling at all. He was a swan!

As the other swans joined him, the happy bird promised himself that he would never forget the things he had learned as an ugly duckling—even though he would now spend the rest of his life as a handsome swan.